JAZZ BABY

Lisa Wheeler

R. Gregory Christie

HARCOURT, INC.

Orlando   Austin   New York   San Diego   Toronto   London

Library of Congress Cataloging-in-Publication Data
Wheeler, Lisa, 1963–
Jazz baby/Lisa Wheeler; illustrated by R. Gregory Christie.
p. cm.
Summary: Baby and his family make some jazzy music.
[1. Babies—Fiction. 2. Music—Fiction.   3. Stories in rhyme.]
I. Christie, Gregory, 1971- ill.   II. Title.
PZ8.3.W5668Jaz   2007
[E]—dc22   2006009236
ISBN 978-0-15-202522-9

H G F E D C B

Manufactured in China

The illustrations in this book were done in gouache.
The display type was set in P22 Cage.
The text type was set in Handegypt.
Color separations by Bright Arts Ltd., Hong Kong
Manufactured by South China Printing Company, Ltd., China
Production supervision by Pascha Gerlinger
Designed by Lauren Rille

For my dad, Dennis Haroulakis,
the jazziest guy I know—L.W.

For Kennedy
and the Lloyd family—R.G.C.

Brother's hands tap.
Sister's hands snap.

Itty-bitty Baby's hands

CLAP-CLAP-CLAP!

Mama sings high.

Daddy sings low.

So they **TOOT-TOOT-TOOT**

and they
SNAP-SNAP-SNAP

and the bouncin' baby bebops
with a
CLAP-
CLAP-
CLAP!

Auntie toe-taps.
Uncle soft-shoes.

Fancy-dancin' Baby sings,

"DOO-WOP-DOO!"

Cousins
BOOM-
BOOM.
Neighbors
hip-hop.

Rompin'-stompin' Baby goes

BOP- BOP- BOP!

Mama swings high.
Daddy swings low.

So they
BOOM-BOOM-BOOM

and they HIP-HIP-HOP

and the bouncin' baby boogies
with a

BOP-

BOP-

BOP!

Snappy-happy Baby goes

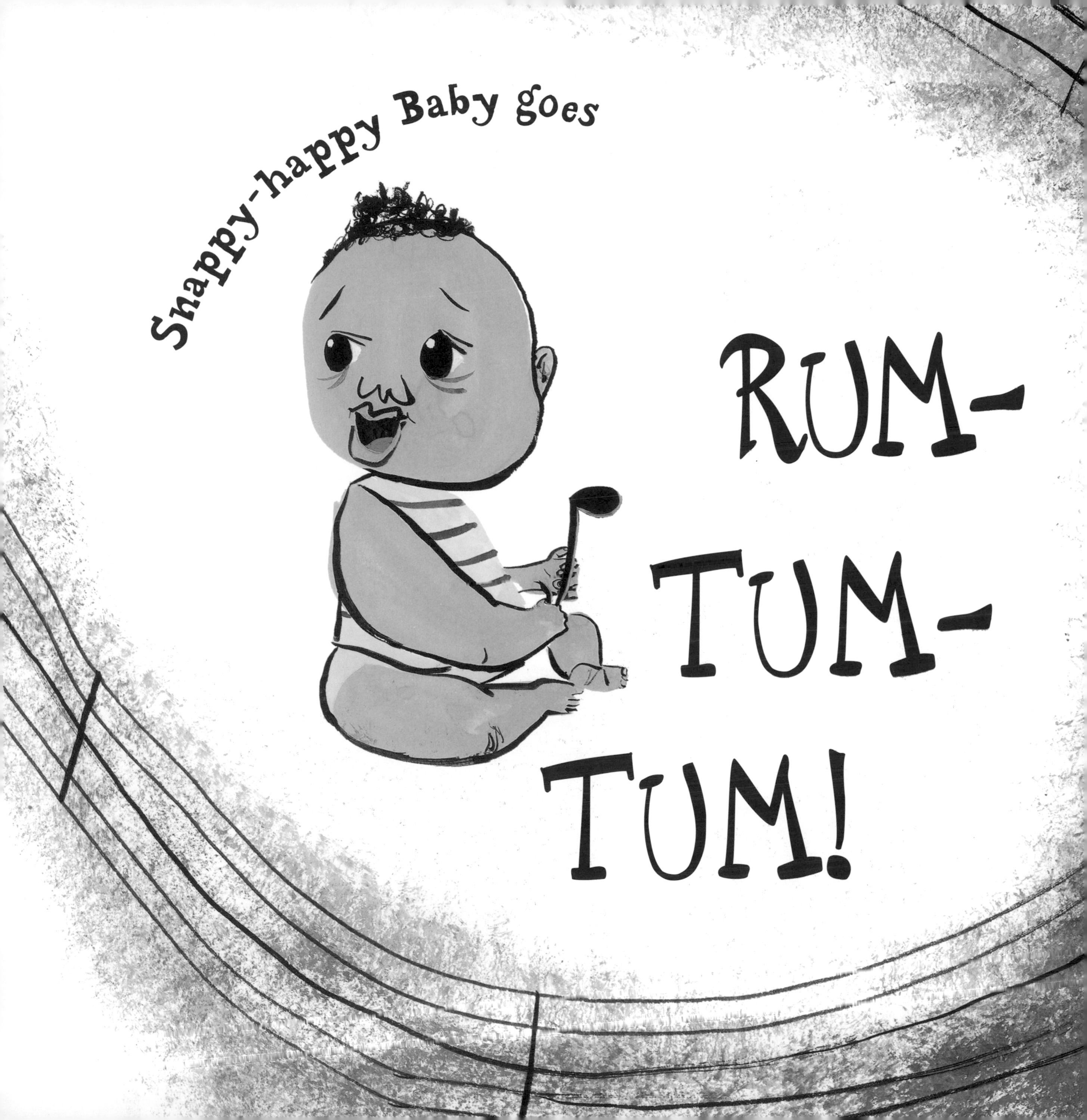

RUM-
TUM-
TUM!

Tempo goes up.
Lights go down.

Busy-dizzy Baby goes round and round!

Daddy jumps high.

Mama bends low.

and the bouncin' baby limbos with a RUM-TUM-TUM!

Brother's arms hold.
Sister's arms hug.
Rock-a-byin' Baby
so warm and snug.

Grandpa smiles wide.

Granny smiles, too.

Drowsy-dozy Baby sings,

"LAA-LAA-LOO."

Daddy sings blues.
Mama sings sweet.

While that snoozy-woozy baby...